"Miles gasped in horror and started sprinting towards the door. He heard a car engine revving as he burst into the street outside.

A hand grabbed him by the throat and threw him onto the back seat of the car. Miles hit his head on something hard inside the car and lost consciousness."

By Royal Order or Death

By Royal Order or Death
by Jonny Zucker
Illustrated by Stuart Harrison

Published by Ransom Publishing Ltd.
Radley House, 8 St. Cross Road, Winchester, Hampshire
SO23 9HX, UK
www.ransom.co.uk

ISBN 978 178127 715 7
First published in 2015

A CIP catalogue record of this book is available from the British Library.

BY ROYAL ORDER OR DEATH

JONNY ZUCKER

ILLUSTRATED BY

STUART HARRISON

CHAPTER 1

A punch came flying towards Miles' face. He blocked it with both hands and launched a kick at Kelvin's stomach. Kelvin parried the blow and hit out.

In an instant, Miles leapt to one side and brought Kelvin crashing to the ground. He followed through and held him there with a steel grip.

'And everyone focus back on me again,' called out Otis.

Miles, Kelvin and the other eight students stood to attention and faced the tiny shaven-headed figure of Otis – their trainer.

'You've been with me for three weeks inside this Royal Protection Youth Hub,' announced Otis.

'In that time you've learned about protecting people at close range, moving people safely in tight spaces, hand-to-hand combat and dealing with weapons. Your training is now over.'

Miles and Kelvin grinned at each other. They'd met on the first day of training and had been regular sparring partners since then.

'Protecting high-profile teenagers of a similar age to you is tough work. It can be boring and repetitive, with long hours – during which you must be on high alert every second.'

Miles pulled a face. Kelvin stifled a laugh.

'However,' went on Otis, 'it can be incredibly exciting and can make a massive difference to people's lives. If you can use your skills to keep those you are protecting out of harm's way, you will have done an excellent job.

'I will now announce who you'll be assigned to.'

'This is where it's going to get interesting,' whispered Miles.

Otis started to read from a list. Kelvin was given a politician's son to protect.

Other people got the kids of celebrities. One girl got a teenage pop star who was known to be *ever so slightly* difficult.

Miles' name was not on the list.

Before Miles could ask what was going on, Otis dismissed the others. Kelvin waved goodbye and then he and the rest of the group were led away.

'Miles,' said Otis, walking over to him. 'As you have trained so well and learned so much in our time together, I am giving you a special assignment.'

'Who is it?' asked Miles.

Otis paused a moment and then said: 'Princess Helena.'

CHAPTER 2

Miles stared at Otis in shock. '*The* Princess Helena?' he asked. 'As in King Azure's daughter?'

'The very one,' smiled Otis. 'I've heard she is a somewhat challenging character and I believe you are the right person to protect her.'

'I'll do my best,' said Miles. He'd seen Princess Helena on TV a few times. She was a couple of months older than him.

'Your car is waiting,' said Otis, shaking Miles' hand. 'I wish you the best of luck.'

*****

Half an hour later, Miles found himself sitting in the back of an impressive black car with tinted windows, driving through several check points and into the secure car park at the back of King Azure's palace.

The driver opened Miles' door and a tall man in a grey suit hurried forward to greet him.

'I'm Christopher Walsh,' he said to Miles, leading him up a flight of steps. 'I look after Princess Helena's day-to-day schedule. She's waiting for you upstairs.'

They took a service lift up four floors and walked out onto a lushly carpeted corridor. Walsh stopped outside a large oak door and rapped on it three times with his knuckles.

'Enter,' came a voice from within.

Mr Walsh opened the door and ushered Miles inside.

Sitting at a huge oak desk sat Princess Helena. She was rapidly tapping on a mobile phone with her long fingernails and muttering to herself.

She was wearing jeans and a grey T-shirt and her hair was squashed on top of her head like a giant bunch of grapes.

Mr Walsh cleared his throat.

'I have Miles Stern here, Princess Helena. He is your new close protection operative.'

'I hope he's better than the last one,' said the princess, looking up from her phone and scowling.

'I'm sure you two will get along fine,' smiled Mr Walsh. 'I'll leave you to get to know each other.'

He backed out of the room and closed the doors behind him.

'Right,' declared Helena. 'This is how it works. You stay as far away from me as possible and when I say *don't follow me*, I mean *don't follow me*. *Especially* at the party tonight.'

'I'm afraid I won't be able to do that, because … ' started Miles, but Princess Helena cut him off.

'I don't care what they taught you at bodyguard school – you will do things MY way from now on. Now go and stand outside the door and make sure no one comes in!'

CHAPTER 3

Miles stood outside the door, trying to control his anger.

Surely, the fact that she was a princess didn't mean that she could speak to him like that.

And as for not following her – that wasn't an option. He was her *close* protection operative; he would stick to her wherever she went, party or no party. His job – and her life – depended on it.

As he stood guard, various people appeared at the door to deliver things to her; some bottled water, a scarf, some throat lozenges. Miles checked all of their ID badges carefully before letting them in.

*****

As night began to fall, Princess Helena emerged from her room, wearing a long blue ball gown and an emerald necklace.

She swept down the corridor and Miles followed. She entered the lift. He stepped in behind her.

'Well go on, press the ground floor button!' she ordered.

Miles pressed the button, wondering why she wasn't able to perform this task herself.

A large party was already in full swing in the palace ballroom. Tables groaning with food and drinks had been set up. Men in smart suits and women in elegant dresses were circling. The sounds of chatter and laughter filled the air.

Miles stayed close to the princess, even though she told him to 'back off' a number of times.

She talked to a few older people, clearly pretending to be interested in what they were saying, and then she made for some double doors at the far end of the room.

Miles stepped after her. She stopped when she'd opened the doors.

Plate

‘What do you think you’re doing?’ she demanded.

‘I’m following you,’ replied Miles. ‘That’s my job and that’s what I’m going to do.’

‘Now listen here, Miles – or whatever your name is. I need to make a private phone call and I will *not* make it with you hanging around me like an annoying shadow.’

Before Miles could reply, Princess Helena slipped outside, through the doors, and started striding down the lawn. Miles stepped out and hurried after her.

‘Go away!’ she hissed, looking over her shoulder and pulling out her mobile phone.

She crossed a small bridge that stood above a gently flowing stream, before disappearing into a thicket of trees.

Miles ran over the bridge and fought his way through the trees. He came out on the other side and spotted Helena leaning against a tree next to a stone wall and talking on her phone.

Five seconds later, two shadowy figures suddenly emerged from a door set into the wall. They grabbed the princess and dragged her through the door.

Miles gasped in horror and started sprinting towards the door. He heard a car engine revving as he burst out onto the street outside.

A hand grabbed him by the throat and threw him onto the back seat of the car, beside the princess. Miles hit his head on something hard inside the car and lost consciousness.

A moment later, the car pulled away from the kerb and shot out into the night.

CHAPTER 4

Feeling groggy, Miles opened his eyes. He was still in the car.

He tried to move, but discovered that both of his wrists were handcuffed and tied to a metal pole in the back seat. Princess Helena's hands were also cuffed in the same way.

'What on EARTH are you doing?' she screamed. 'I am a PRINCESS! Let me go immediately!'

But the two figures in the front said nothing.

Miles tried desperately to release himself from the handcuffs, but it was impossible.

He looked out of the window as the car left the packed streets of the city and sped into the countryside. Past fields and hills they hurtled, until they reached a high mountain.

A single-track road wound its way up the mountain and at the top one of the men got out and unlocked a concealed gate. He waved the car through, locked the gate and climbed back inside.

The car then followed a narrow windy stone path onto a large tarmac concourse. At the end stood a low building carved into the rock of the mountainside.

The men parked the car and got out. For the first time, Miles could get a proper look at them. One man was broad-shouldered with a thick beard; the other was sinewy and tall, with a scar on his left cheek.

The bearded one opened the back door, undid Helena's handcuffs from the metal pole and pulled her out.

'GET OFF ME!' she screamed.

'Keep the noise down,' he snarled, 'or you won't last five minutes here.'

Scar-face released Miles' handcuffs from the pole and dragged him out of the car. The men then tied Miles and Helena's handcuffs together. This meant they had to walk very close to each other, which neither of them was too pleased about.

The men hurried them through some glass double-doors and then down two flights of stairs.

'My father will do you for TREASON!' screeched Princess Helena furiously.

The men totally ignored her.

Miles listened to the two men talking in low whispers. He couldn't make out what they were talking about, but he discovered that the bearded man's name was Red and the other guy was Frank. He had no idea whether these were their real names or not.

At the bottom of the stairs was a large brown door. Red shielded his hand and

pressed some numbers on a wall-mounted panel. The door slid open.

'Welcome to your new home,' announced Frank. 'We hope you'll be comfortable here.'

He undid the handcuffs and pocketed them. Then he reached into a pocket of Helena's ball gown and grabbed her mobile phone. He pulled out the SIM card and held it in his hand, while he dropped the rest of the phone on the floor and stamped on it.

'Hey!' shouted an alarmed Helena. 'That's a royal phone. You can't just destroy it!'

Frank scowled at her and then he and Red hurried out of the room, sliding the door shut behind them.

Miles and Princess Helena were truly trapped.

CHAPTER 5

'This is all your fault,' snapped Helena, slumping to the floor.

'My fault?' gasped Miles. '*You* were the one who ran off to the bottom of the garden and tried to lose me.'

'It was a PRIVATE phone call!' whined Helena.

'Well it's a phone call that has got us into a mound of trouble,' replied Miles tersely.

He paced around the room, trying to collect his thoughts. Who were these men and why had they snatched Helena? Was it just for money, or was there something else going on?

'I should have told that idiot Walsh to get rid of you the moment I saw you,' grumbled Helena.

'Do you EVER say ANYTHING positive?' snapped Miles. 'Do you ever smile or do something good, or do you always just moan and whine as if the world was designed with the specific purpose of serving you?'

This seemed to knock the wind out of Helena's sails for a few moments and she sat there sulking.

Miles used this break in hostilities to check the door. It was reinforced with steel and was shut very firmly.

He walked to the two small windows and pulled at the metal bars covering them. They wouldn't budge. In the corner he found a pile of old bits of wood, empty paint tins and some other discarded items.

He kicked a paint tin in frustration. He'd let the princess be taken on his watch, and on his first evening as well. Otis would kill him!

He knocked at several places on the walls, but there were no hollow replies. The walls were very thick. He gazed up at the high ceiling, but without a ladder or some chairs he'd never be able to get up there.

He sat on the floor facing Helena.

'I'm hungry,' moaned the princess. 'When will they feed us?'

'Maybe they won't feed us,' said Miles.

*****

They sat, lost in their own thoughts, for over an hour. Then they saw the door sliding open. Red and Frank appeared and told them to get up.

'It's time for the tour,' declared Red. 'There's something we want to show you.'

Miles and Helena looked at each other in confusion.

'Well hurry up,' said Frank, 'we haven't got all day.'

He pushed them outside.

Miles and Helena walked slowly down the corridor, with Red and Frank right behind them.

'Don't try any funny stuff,' said Red in a menacing voice. 'If you do, you'll seriously regret it.'

Miles swallowed anxiously and, with the princess at his side, walked on down the corridor.

CHAPTER 6

They passed several green doors, a water-cooler and two tired-looking plants. They saw a row of metal cabinets, some desks with laptops on them and a thick tangle of electrical cables.

Finally they passed under a white archway, walked through some black double doors and entered a laboratory. There were several computer screens fixed to the walls and three banks of silver machinery.

In the far corner was a long metal box. It was about Miles' height and it rested horizontally on a long wooden bench.

'What is this place?' mouthed Miles.

'Whatever it is, I demand a hot bath and a five-course meal,' declared Helena. 'And I also demand a decent bed. There is no way I am sleeping on the floor of that awful white room.'

'You know what?' said Frank irritably. 'You talk too much. It's high time you kept your mouth shut and listened to someone else for a change.'

Miles thought about saying he totally agreed with Frank, but he decided against this course of action. However annoying

Helena was, it was his job to keep her safe. He'd already failed once at this task; he'd have to do way better here.

'Come and see your sister,' said Red, directing them both towards the bench and the box.

'I don't have a sister,' said Helena. 'I have two brothers and they are both right royal pains.'

'OK,' grinned Red when they'd reached the box. 'Be prepared for an introduction.'

Miles and Helena peered into the box. Its top was covered with thousands of white polystyrene balls, the kind that are packaged with new washing machines.

Red pressed some buttons on a black, handheld remote panel.

The polystyrene balls started moving, slowly at first, but gradually getting quicker. They looked like water bubbling in a pan.

Red pressed another button and, throwing the polystyrene balls aside, Princess Helena sat up in the box and beamed a radiant smile.

CHAPTER 7

Suddenly there were two 'Princess Helenas' in the room. Miles and the Princess Helena standing next to him took a few steps back in horror.

'This is Sky,' said Red, pressing some buttons on the remote panel.

The second Princess Helena climbed out of the box and stood facing them.

'I am under the control of my masters, Red and Frank,' she announced.

'W … w … what's going on?' mouthed the visibly shaken real Helena.

Sky turned to face the princess.

'I am going to be your replacement, Helena,' said Sky in an exact replica of Helena's voice. 'Soon I will be ready and I will travel to your palace.

'Your father and everybody else at the palace will not be able to tell the difference between you and I. This is Red and Frank's genius scheme.'

'You're crazy! You can't do this!' snapped Miles. 'They'll all realise it's not the real Helena.'

'Oh really?' said Sky.

Suddenly she burst into song, singing Helena's favourite tune, note-perfect in every respect. Then she stood on her tiptoes and performed one of Helena's short ballet sequences. The moves were exact.

Finally she recited a poem, using her voice in the precise way Helena did.

'No one will be able to tell us apart,' declared Sky, with a smile that was identical to Helena's.

'But what will happen to me?' asked Helena quietly.

'You?' replied Sky. 'While modifications are being made to me you are of use, but when I am complete there will be no need for your existence.'

'This is ridiculous!' hissed Miles. 'And I've had enough.'

He lunged forward and shoved Sky hard in the chest, knocking her back into her box. Then he floored Red with a punch on the side of his cheek.

This left Frank.

Miles adopted a fighting stance, sure that with his training he could beat Frank. He was right. After they'd traded a couple of blows, Miles was still standing strong, but Frank was dizzy and swaying from side to side.

Miles was about to knock Frank out when Sky suddenly shot forward and squeezed Miles on the neck.

There was a loud fizzing sound and a spark of electricity, before Miles' legs gave way and he dropped onto the floor.

CHAPTER 8

'Well this is just great!' groaned Helena, slumping to the floor and sitting with her back against the wall.

She and Miles were back in the cell.

'First you get me kidnapped, then you get an electric shock from my terrifying electrical body double and ruin our chance of ever making it out of here.'

'Can you stop moaning for one second!' snapped Miles. 'We still have a chance to get out before they dispose of you and replace you with Sky.'

'Can't you see there's no way out?' scowled Helena. 'We're doomed in here.'

Miles gritted his teeth and walked over to the large pile of stuff in the corner. There were old clothes, chunks of wood, some off-cuts of carpet, empty paint tins and lengths of rope.

He studied everything for a couple of minutes and then smiled.

Quickly he started grabbing items. He took some lengths of wood and lashed them together with pieces of rope. He added more wood and a number of paint tins.

Helena tried to show no interest in his activities, but curiosity got the better of her.

'This is no time for Lego,' she said sourly. 'What are you doing?'

Miles ignored her and continued working.

Ten minutes later he stood his invention upright. It was a makeshift ladder.

He stood on the first rung and it broke. Grabbing some more rope he fixed it and, literally step by step, he made the ladder steadier until he could reach the top and touch the ceiling.

'You look ridiculous,' observed Helena.

‘At least I’m doing something other than sitting there and whingeing,’ Miles shot back.

‘How *dare* you talk to me like that?’ shouted Helena.

But Miles was already busy, pressing the ceiling tiles and seeing if any of them would budge.

The first ten he tried would not shift, but the eleventh came loose and fell to the floor. Above it were strips of metal.

He pulled down several other tiles and then he struck gold. One of them covered a small wire vent. He moved this from side to side until it came away. There was now a small opening in the ceiling.

Gripping the sides, Miles pulled himself up and found himself in a small metal tunnel.

He turned around and poked his head down through the hole.

'I think I've found an escape route!' he called to Princess Helena.

CHAPTER 9

'There is no way I'm going into some disgusting tunnel!' snapped Helena, folding her arms.

'Fine!' snapped back Miles. 'Stay there, be killed and let a robot replace you! See if *I* care!'

Helena let out a squeal of fury, stamped her foot several times and then shinned up the makeshift ladder. Miles crawled forward and Helena slotted in close behind him.

'It stinks,' complained Helena, holding her nose in disgust at the musty, damp smell.

Miles rolled his eyes and moved on as quickly as he could. It was hot in the tunnel and crawling space was very limited, but they both had just about enough room to keep going.

Helena muttered furiously under her breath. Miles ignored her.

*****

They'd been going for about fifteen minutes when Miles came across a vent on the floor. He looked down and saw an empty corridor

with a couple of doors on one side. He listened but couldn't hear a sound.

Slowly and as silently as possible, he pulled the vent off, laid it on the floor of the tunnel and lowered himself through the hole. He let go and fell to the floor, landing on his feet.

'Come on!' he hissed, 'Get down here.'

'I've told you before about issuing orders to me!' snarled Helena. 'I'm the one who gives the orders round here.'

'Fine!' snapped Miles. 'Well give yourself an order to jump down here.'

Helena scowled at him and then pushed her legs through the hole and let herself go, landing right next to Miles.

Miles hurried over to a window.

'Look,' he said, 'that's the front of the building. If we go down a floor we'll be able to get out and make a run for it.'

'That was what I was going to say,' whined Helena.

'It doesn't matter who said it, let's just do it,' replied Miles.

They crept through a couple of doors and began climbing down a narrow steel staircase.

But just before they reached the blue door at the bottom, it swung open and there stood Frank and Red.

Frank took one look at Helena, then ran towards her, raised his fist and brought it crashing down towards her face.

CHAPTER 10

As Frank's fist neared its target, Helena blocked it with her left arm and punched Frank hard in the stomach. He yelped out in pain and went crashing backwards onto the floor.

Helena then spun round and caught Red in the throat with a powerful high kick. He

crumpled to the ground and fell on top of Frank. The two of them lay there moaning.

Miles looked at Helena in astonishment.

'What?' she scowled.

'I didn't know you had it in you,' he said.

'Nor did I,' she snapped. 'Now let's get out of here.'

They ran through the blue door and out into the lobby. Miles hit a green EXIT button and the large glass front door opened automatically.

Emerging outside into the fresh air, they saw a low perimeter wall. That was when they saw the helicopter. It was several hundred metres away, but was heading in their direction.

'It's got the royal crest!' cried Helena. 'It must be a rescue mission! About time, too!'

As soon as she'd said this, there was the crack of a gun being fired, and a bullet rushed through the air. It sped narrowly past them and lodged itself in a wall.

Miles spun round and saw Sky. She was standing on the roof of the building, holding a giant silver gun with telescopic sights.

She aimed at Miles and Helena and pulled the trigger again.

'MOVE!' yelled Miles, pushing Helena in the back. A second bullet whizzed past their heads.

'Don't push me! I'm a princess!' shrieked Helena.

'I just saved your life!' shouted Miles. 'Now RUN!'

They sprinted towards the perimeter wall as bullets flew all around them.

'YOU HAVE TO DIE SO THAT I CAN LIVE!' roared Sky, releasing another volley of bullets.

Miles grabbed Helena by the arm and zig-zagged as they ran to avoid being struck by the deadly fire.

The helicopter was now overhead and Miles could see three men in black suits and dark glasses. One of them poked a sniper's rifle out of a window and fired at Sky.

One second she was there, the next she was lying on the floor.

The helicopter reached the ground and the sniper motioned Miles and Helena towards it.

They vaulted over the low wall and raced across a stretch of tarmac.

The door flew open. The royal sniper grabbed the princess and pulled her in, quickly followed by Miles.

'To the palace!' instructed the sniper.

The pilot started his preflight routine and the helicopter rose majestically into the air.

'How did you find us?' asked Helena over the roar of the rotors.

'Even though they broke your phone, we managed to pick up your signal about twenty minutes ago,' replied the sniper. 'We didn't want to storm in there and get you killed, but we thought that time might be running out.'

Helena sighed deeply. She wasn't impressed by this explanation.

'You did well to save the princess, Miles,' noted the sniper.

'*Save* me?' yelled Helena. 'He did NOTHING! *I* saved HIM.'

Miles couldn't believe what he was hearing. After all they'd been through together, she was still prepared to tell a bare-faced lie just to shame him.

But the corners of Helena's mouth twitched, and a few seconds later her face broke out into a smile.

'Only joking,' she grinned. 'Without him I'd be dead.'

Miles looked at her in shock. It looked like she might be human after all.

'Not bad for a first day in the job, Miles,' nodded the sniper.

'So long as every day's not like this,' hit back Miles.

Princess Helena couldn't stop herself from smiling.

TOXIC

Now read the first chapter of another great Toxic title by Jonny Zucker:

CHAPTER 1

'WHAT'S HAPPENING?' yelled Jed, as the gleaming silver spaceship stopped for a moment and then suddenly started to nose-dive.

Mr Graham, Jed and the other three kids – Tariq, Jodie and Carla – were flung around like bullets, smashing into each other and against the walls.

'SEATBELTS! IMMEDIATELY!' barked Mr Graham.

The five of them were flung left and right, up and down, but they all managed to reach the seat harnesses and put them on.

Jed saw stars and dust clouds rush past the windows as the spaceship got faster and faster.

He couldn't believe it.

He was one of the first five people chosen to visit Mars, the famous *red planet*, and now their spaceship was going to crash, only seven days after take-off and millions of miles from their destination.

'WE'VE LOST THREE ENGINES!' shouted Mr Graham, pressing buttons and pulling levers desperately.

Jed felt an icy bolt of fear in his chest. The spaceship only had three engines! If they'd all gone, this mission and its passengers would be toast.

A piercing alarm started ringing every few seconds, its horrible electronic tune belting out its terrible news.

'WE'RE ALL GOING TO DIE!' screamed Tariq.

The ship tilted violently to the left, but the seatbelts held firm.

'ADOPT THE BRACE POSITION!' ordered Mr Graham, covering his head with his hands and arms.

The children immediately copied him. *We've been trained for this kind of emergency*, thought Jed. *But I never thought we'd need to use these skills*.

The ship was going incredibly fast and, as well as the noise of the alarm, it was now making a horrible high-pitched whistling sound, like a furious kettle.

'We're entering the atmosphere!' shouted Mr Graham.

Outside, the black of space had changed to a sky-blue colour.

Jed was pretty sure that Tariq was right. These were going to be his last few moments of life.

He thought about his parents and his little sister, Lilly. He'd never see them again. He'd never again hear Dad's crummy jokes, Mum's impressions of famous celebrities or Lilly's crazy singing.

'PREPARE FOR IMPACT!' shrieked Mr Graham.

Five seconds later, the craft hit the ground with a gigantic booming sound.

The next thing Jed knew was blackness.

TOXIC

MORE GREAT TOXIC READS

Action-packed adventure stories featuring jungles, swamps, deserted islands, robots, space travel, zombies, computer viruses and monsters from the deep.

How many have you read?

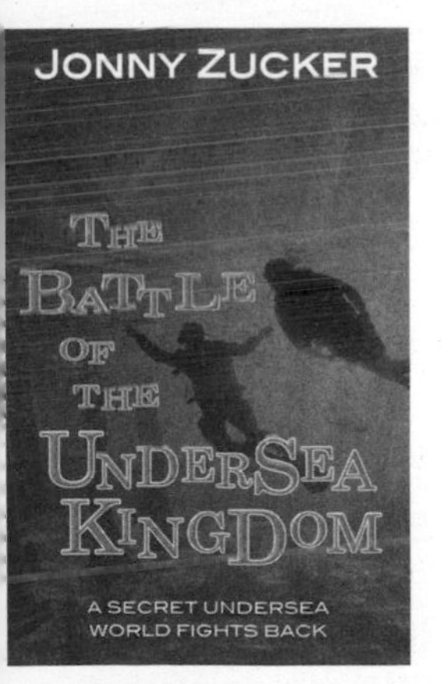

THE BATTLE OF THE UNDERSEA KINGDOM

by Jonny Zucker

When the local mayor is kidnapped, the people suspect other villages of taking him. But Danny's dad, Tyler, knows more. He thinks that creatures from under the sea are to blame – and he's going to prove it!

MORE GREAT TOXIC READS

FOOTBALL FORCE

by Jonny Zucker

It's 2066 and football has changed. Players now wear lightweight body armour. Logan Smith wants to play for the best local team – Vestige United. Their players are fantastic, but Logan suspects that the team has a dark secret.

ISLAND SHOCK

by Jonny Zucker

Mike Chen wakes up on a deserted beach. The last thing he remembers is waiting for a flight at the airport. How did he get here? Where are his friends? Mike soon realises that he is surrounded by danger on all sides. Can he survive the attacks of wild creatures and find out what is going on?

More Great Toxic Reads

Gladiator Revival

by Jonny Zucker

Nick and Kat are on holiday in Rome with their parents. So how do they end up facing the perils of the Coliseum in ancient Rome – as gladiators? Is somebody making a film? Or is this for real and they are fighting for their lives?

Crash Land Earth

by Jonny Zucker

Jed and his friends are setting out on a trip to Mars. But their spaceship is in trouble and they are forced to crash-land back on Earth. But nothing is quite as it should be. Jed and his fellow explorers find themselves in a race against time to save planet Earth.

Jonny Zucker has been a teacher, musician, stand-up comedian and footballer, but now he is best known as one of the most popular authors for children. So far he has written over 100 books.

Jonny also plays in a band and has done over 60 gigs as a stand-up comedian, reaching the London Region Final of the BBC New Comedy awards.

He still dreams of being a professional footballer.